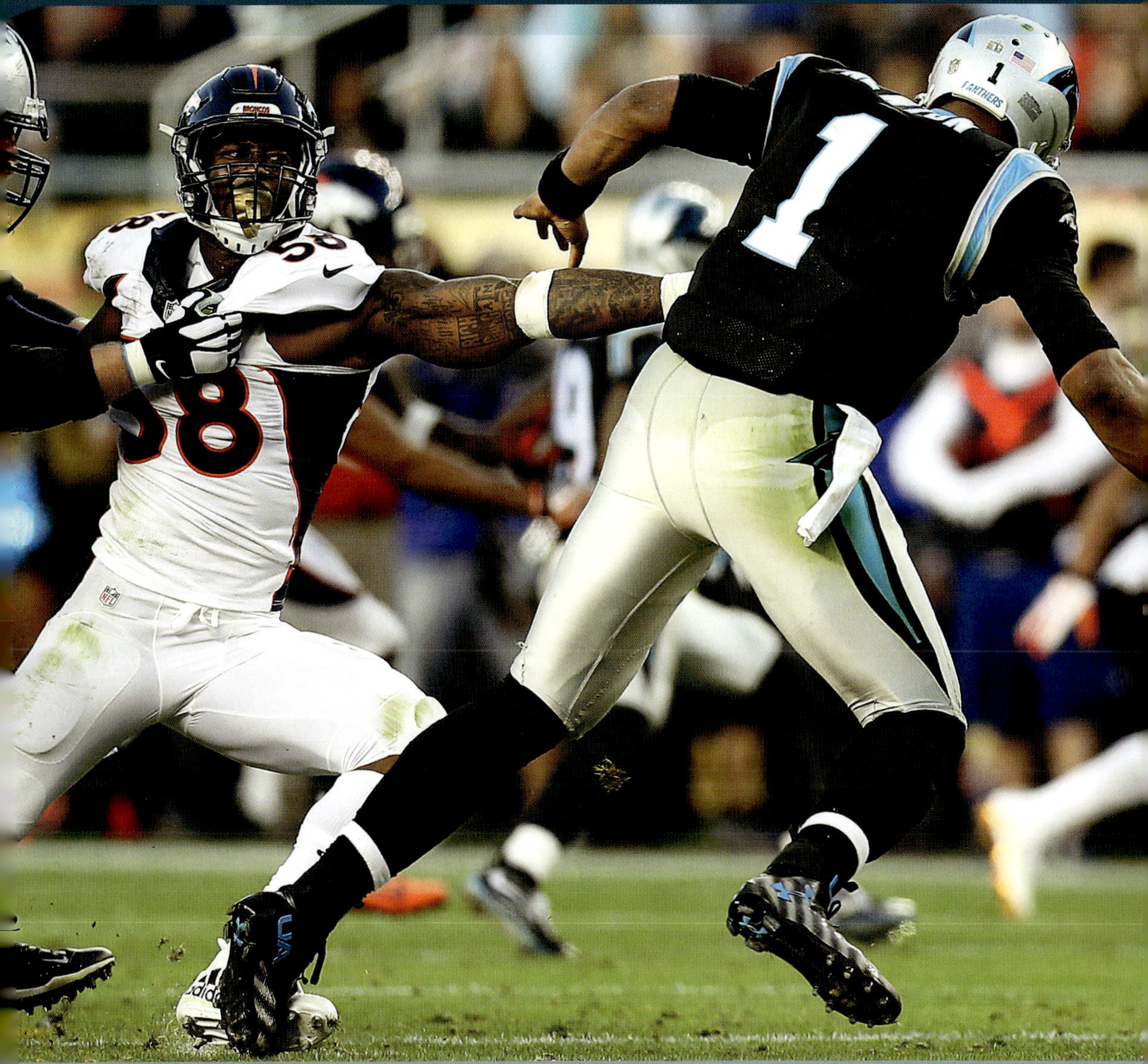

# BIGGEST SUPER BOWL UPSETS

by Paul Bowker

www.12StoryLibrary.com



12-Story Library is an imprint of Bookstaves.

Photographs ©: Doug Benc/Associated Press, cover, 1; Associated Press, 4; Florida Memory/PD, 5; PD, 5; Associated Press, 6; PD, 7; Al Messerschmidt/Associated Press, 8; PD, 9; Tony Tomsic/Associated Press, 9; Kevin Reece/Icon Sportswire/Associated Press, 10; Jeffrey Beall/CC2.0, 11; PD, 11; Kevin Reece/Icon Sportswire/Associated Press, 12; PD, 13; Kevin Terrell/Associated Press, 14; Al Messerschmidt/Associated Press, 15; PD, 15; Mark J. Terrill/Associated Press, 16; Paul Spinelli/Associated Press, 17; PD, 17; Ben Liebenberg/Associated Press, 18; Ted Kerwin/CC2.0, 19; PD, 19; Dick Druckman/Associated Press, 20; Ian Ransley/CC2.0, 21; PD, 21; Marcio Sanchez/Associated Press, 22; Austin Kirk/CC2.0, 23; PD, 23; Paul Sancya/Associated Press, 24; Anthony Quintano/CC2.0, 25; PD, 25; Charlie Riedel/Associated Press, 26; Arnie Papp/CC2.0, 27; PD, 27; US EPA, 28; Capt. Darin Overstreet/US Air National Guard, 29

**ISBN**
978-1-63235-547-8 (hardcover)
978-1-63235-665-9 (ebook)

**Library of Congress Control Number: 2018948079**

Printed in the United States of America
Mankato, MN
June 2018

# Table of Contents

1

# Super Bowl III: New York Jets vs. Baltimore Colts

The Green Bay Packers won the first two Super Bowls in 1967 and 1968. In the early days of the Super Bowl the professional football teams were known as the National Football League and American Football League. The older franchises were in the NFL. The NFL division held both Super Bowl titles.

Quarterback Joe Namath and the New York Jets changed everything. Three days before the game Namath guaranteed that the Jets would win. The claim was met with ridicule. The Baltimore Colts were 18-point favorites. But on January 12, 1969, Namath kept his word. He passed for 206 yards. The Jets shocked the pro football world by knocking off the Colts by a 16 to 7 score. Namath was named game Most Valuable Player (MVP). Namath grabbed the headlines. But the Jets running game and defense won the game. Matt Snell of the Jets rushed for 121 yards and a touchdown. Jim Turner kicked three field goals.

## BROADWAY JOE GUARANTEE

New York Jets quarterback Joe Namath was a brash young quarterback. He came from the University of Alabama. And was known as Broadway Joe. He was speaking to the Miami Touchdown Club when he made his famous guarantee: to win Super Bowl III. Namath backed up his words with a historic victory. He never played in the Super Bowl again. He was inducted into the Pro Football Hall of Fame in 1985.

**43**

**Number of running plays by the New York Jets.**

- Jets quarterback Joe Namath passed for 206 yards.
- He became the first AFL player to win the Super Bowl MVP award.
- The Jets became the first AFL team to win the Super Bowl.
- Jets running back Matt Snell rushed for 121 yards and one touchdown.

2

# Super Bowl IV: Kansas City Chiefs vs. Minnesota Vikings

The Kansas City Chiefs struck gold for the American Football League in 1970. The Chiefs lost to the Green Bay Packers by 25 points in Super Bowl I in 1967. Three years later at Super Bowl IV, the Chiefs were 13-point underdogs to the Minnesota Vikings. But Chiefs quarterback Len Dawson picked apart the Vikings defense. He passed for 142 yards and a touchdown. He was named the game MVP.

Jan Stenerud kicked three field goals and two extra points. The Chiefs made three interceptions and recovered two fumbles. The game was a huge victory for the Chiefs since they had lost the first Super Bowl. And had finished second to the Oakland Raiders in the AFL West division in 1969.

The chiefs were thrilled with their first Super Bowl victory. Head coach Hank Stram was carried off the field atop the shoulders of his players.

SUPER BOWL IV

TULANE STADIUM • NEW ORLEANS
JANUARY 11, 1970

# 3

**Number of sacks by the Chiefs of the Vikings quarterback.**

- Chiefs quarterback Len Dawson passed for 142 yards and one touchdown.
- He was named game MVP.
- The Chiefs defense had three interceptions and recovered two Vikings fumbles.
- The Chiefs were the second AFL team to win the Super Bowl.

## SUPER BOWL AT 34

Len Dawson was 34 years old. He led the Kansas City Chiefs to the Super Bowl IV championship. Success for Dawson began late in his career. He was a star quarterback at Purdue University. Then he spent the first five years of his pro career with the Pittsburgh Steelers and Cleveland Browns. He joined the Dallas Texans at age 27. The Dallas team became the Kansas City Chiefs. Dawson led the Chiefs to two Super Bowls and three AFL West titles in six years.

# 3 Super Bowl XXV: New York Giants vs. Buffalo Bills

The Buffalo Bills entered their first Super Bowl game in 1991 on a roll. They had the highest-scoring offense in the NFL. The Bills scored 428 points in 16 games during the regular season. They scored 44 points in a playoff win over the Miami Dolphins. And they scored 51 points in the AFC championship against the Los Angeles Raiders.

The game would become well known for a missed field goal. Buffalo kicker Scott Norwood missed with four seconds left. The kick is known

Hostetler hands the ball off to running back Anderson.

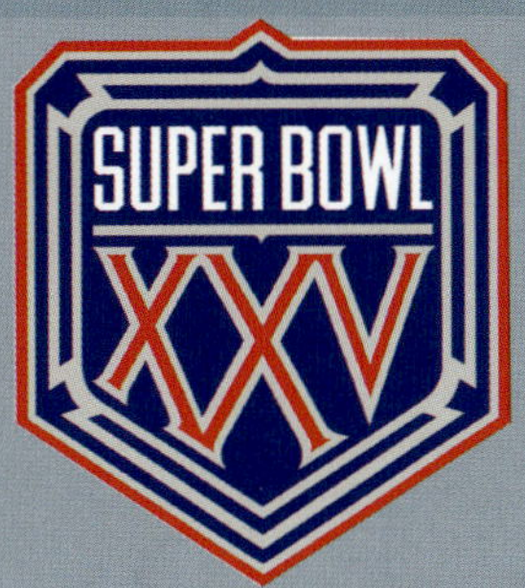


**21**

**Yards kicked by Matt Bahr for a field goal. It won Super Bowl XXV for the New York Giants.**

- The Bills entered the game with the highest-scoring offense in the NFL.
- The Giants slowed the Buffalo Bills by controlling the ball for more than forty minutes.
- Bills kicker Scott Norwood missed a 47-yard field goal.

## USA DAY

Super Bowl XXV was played 10 days after American forces took part in the Persian Gulf War. The game took on a patriotic flavor not seen before. Fans waved American flags. Whitney Houston sang a memorable version of the Star-Spangled Banner. A flyover of F-16 jets preceded the game. "It's stuff you don't forget," said Giants quarterback Jeff Hostetler.

as the "wide right" kick. It allowed the Giants to beat the Bills, 20 to 19.

The Giants beat the Bills with a backup quarterback. Giants starter Phil Simms was injured in a 17 to 13 loss to the Bills during the regular season. Jeff Hostetler took over. He led the Giants to a Super Bowl championship season. Giants running back Ottis Anderson was named Super Bowl MVP. He ran for 102 yards and one touchdown. He was not the leading rusher in the game. That honor went to Thurman Thomas of Buffalo.

4

# Super Bowl XXXII: Denver Broncos vs. Green Bay Packers

Life was grand for the Green Bay Packers in 1997. They were the defending Super Bowl champions. The had beaten the New England Patriots in Super Bowl XXXI that year. They won their third consecutive NFC Central championship. Their star quarterback was Brett Favre.

But an unlikely hero rose up for the Denver Broncos in Super Bowl XXXII. Broncos quarterback John Elway was still trying to win his first Super Bowl game after three tries. No team from the American Football

Conference had won the Super Bowl in 14 years.

The Broncos turned to running back Terrell Davis. Davis rushed for three touchdowns. He won the game for the Broncos on a touchdown run of one yard. It came with one minute, 45 seconds left in the game. Favre then led the Packers to the Denver 35-yard line. But a pass on fourth down fell incomplete. The Broncos defeated the Packers, 31 to 24. Davis was named game MVP. The victory gave Elway his first Super Bowl ring.

**256**

**Yards passed by Packers quarterback Brett Favre in Super Bowl XXXII.**

- Broncos running back Terrell Davis ran for three touchdowns. It was a Super Bowl record.
- The Broncos won the Super Bowl for the first time in team history.
- The Broncos were the first American Football Conference team in 14 years to win the Super Bowl.

## THINK ABOUT IT

Green Bay coach Mike Holmgren instructed his defense to allow the Broncos to score with 1:45 left in the game. This left the Packers more time with which to try to score the tying touchdown. Was this the best strategy? What would you have done?

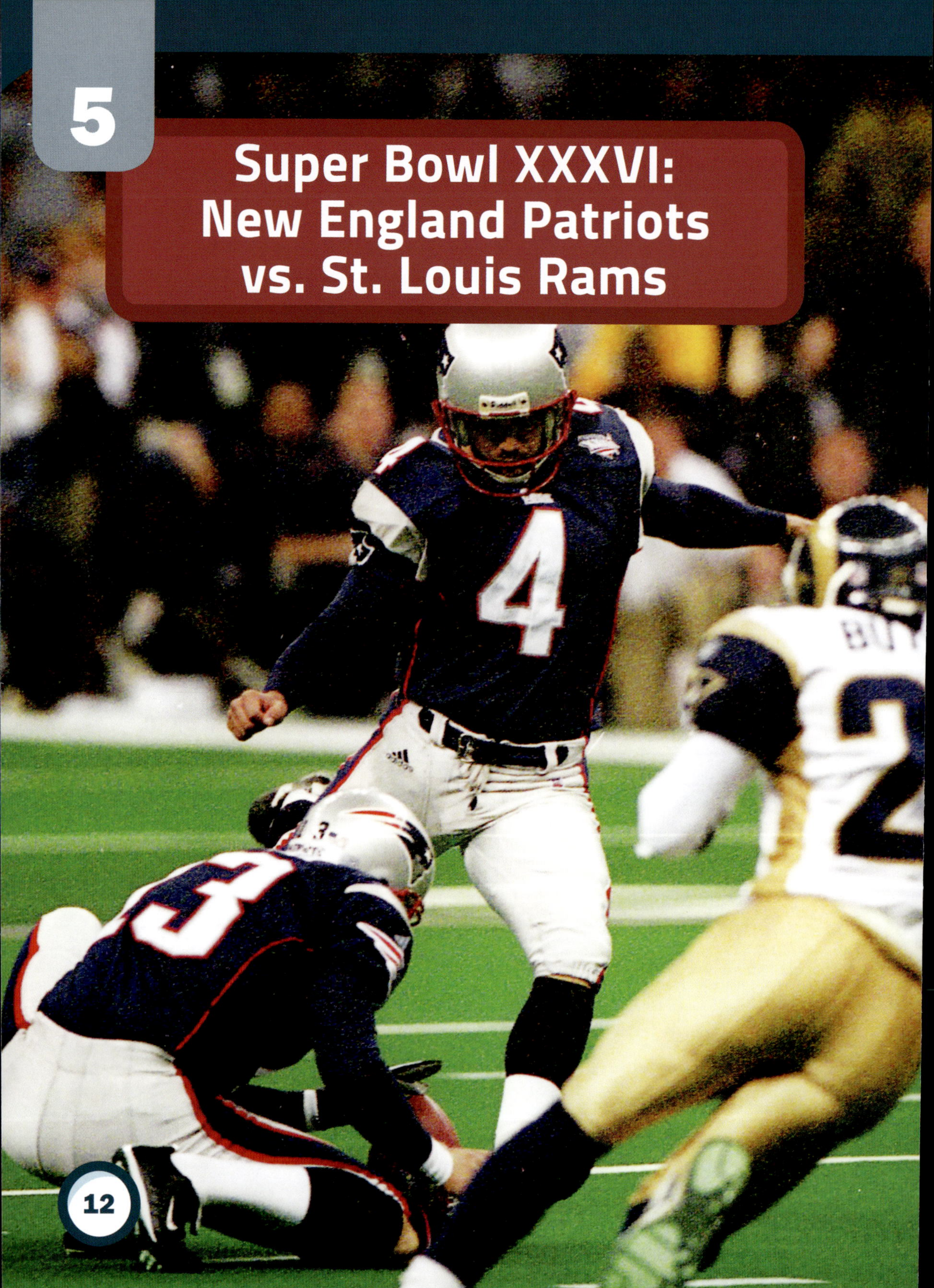

5

# Super Bowl XXXVI: New England Patriots vs. St. Louis Rams

The New England Patriots and quarterback Tom Brady were an unknown in 2002. Super Bowl XXXVI marked the beginning of a historic run. The Patriots were seeking their first Super Bowl victory. They arrived in New Orleans in February of 2002. Brady made his Super Bowl debut. Coach Bill Belichick was trying to win a Super Bowl for the first time as a head coach.

Their opponent was the St. Louis Rams. Quarterback Kurt Warner was named National Football League MVP. He led the Rams to 14 wins during the regular season. They had won their third consecutive NFC West title. But the Patriots pulled off a stunning upset.

The score was tied at 17 to 17 with one minute, 30 seconds left in the game. Brady led the Patriots down the field. He directed a drive from the Patriots 17-yard line to the Rams 30-yard line. It set up the winning kick. Adam Vinatieri kicked a 48-yard field goal on the last play of the game. It gave the Patriots a 20 to 17 win. Brady passed for a total 145 yards. And was named MVP in his first Super Bowl.

**85**

**Yards kicked for two field goals by Patriots kicker Adam Vinatieri in Super Bowl XXXVI.**

- Vinatieri kicked a 48-yard field goal on the final play.
- Patriots won their first Super Bowl.
- Patriots quarterback Tom Brady passed for 145 yards and one touchdown. He was named MVP.
- The Rams had won Super Bowl XXXIV. And they won the NFC West title for the third straight year.

# 6

# Super Bowl XXXVII: Tampa Bay Bucs vs. Oakland Raiders

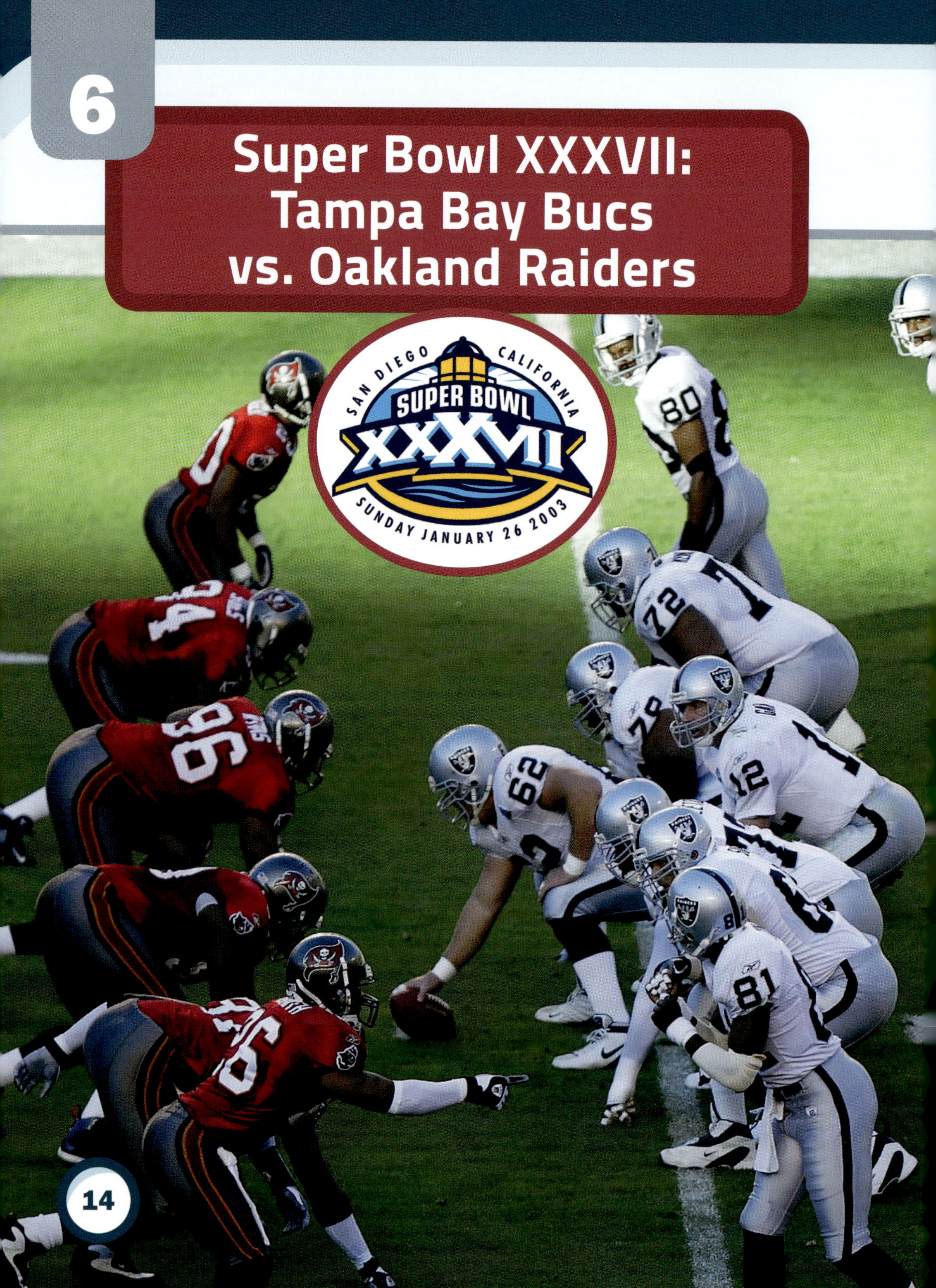

Super Bowl XXXVII may always be remembered as the "Chucky" game. Jon Gruden coached with a scowl. He was often referred to as Chucky, the doll from movie horror fame. Gruden had been coach of the Oakland Raiders when Tampa Bay lured him away. Gruden led the Bucs to their first Super Bowl game in 2003. And it was against the Oakland Raiders.

The Bucs blasted the Raiders. Tampa Bay won 48 to 21. Gruden became the youngest head coach in history to win the Super Bowl at age 39.

But it was really defense that won the Super Bowl for the Bucs. Dexter Jackson had two interceptions. And was named Super Bowl MVP. Dwight Smith also had two interceptions. He returned one interception 50 yards for a touchdown in the fourth quarter. Derrick Brooks returned an interception 44 yards for a touchdown. And the Bucs sacked the Raiders quarterback five times.

## A LONG WAIT

The victory in Super Bowl XXXVII was a reason to celebrate in Tampa Bay. The championship came 26 years after they entered the National Football League. The Buccaneers lost their first 26 games in 1976 and 1977. Their first winning season came in 1979. Jon Gruden arrived as head coach in 2002. And that became the first Super Bowl year for the Bucs.

**5**

**Number of interceptions made by the Buccaneers.**

- Bucs coach Jon Gruden was 39 years old. He became the youngest head coach at the time to win a Super Bowl.
- Tampa Bay Bucs had a strong defensive effort.
- Dexter Jackson had two interceptions. He was selected game MVP.
- Bucs won their first Super Bowl.

7

# Super Bowl XL: Pittsburgh Steelers vs. Seattle Seahawks

The Pittsburgh Steelers rose up as a wild-card playoff team in 2005. They began the playoffs with a wild-card win over the Cincinnati Bengals. Two more wins put them in Super Bowl XL against the Seattle Seahawks in 2006.

The Seahawks were in the Super Bowl for the first time. They had scored more points (452) than any other team in the National

Wide receiver Hines Ward makes a 43-yard touchdown.

Football League. The Steelers held the Seahawks to one touchdown. The Steelers quarterback Ben Roethlisberger was intercepted twice. But the Steelers still defeated the Seahawks 21 to 10.

Jerome Bettis played the final game of his career in Super Bowl XL. He was a running back for the Pittsburgh Steelers. Bettis rushed for 43 yards. It was his only Super Bowl. Wide receiver Hines Ward of the Steelers ended the day with a touchdown catch. It covered 43 yards. He had five catches in the game. He was named game MVP.

**123**

**Passing yards by Pittsburgh Steelers quarterback Ben Roethlisberger.**

- Steelers held the high-powered offense of the Seahawks to one touchdown.
- Jerome Bettis won a Super Bowl in his final game.
- Hines Ward had five catches for 123 yards and a touchdown. He was named game MVP.

## SLEEPLESS IN SEATTLE

It isn't often a referee will say he made the wrong call in a Super Bowl game. Bill Leavy did so. The referee said four years after the game that an incorrect call led to sleepless nights. Leavy said he did the best he could in the game. But he also said it wasn't good enough. Several penalties in the game against the Seahawks were controversial.

# 8 Super Bowl XLII: New York Giants vs. New England Patriots

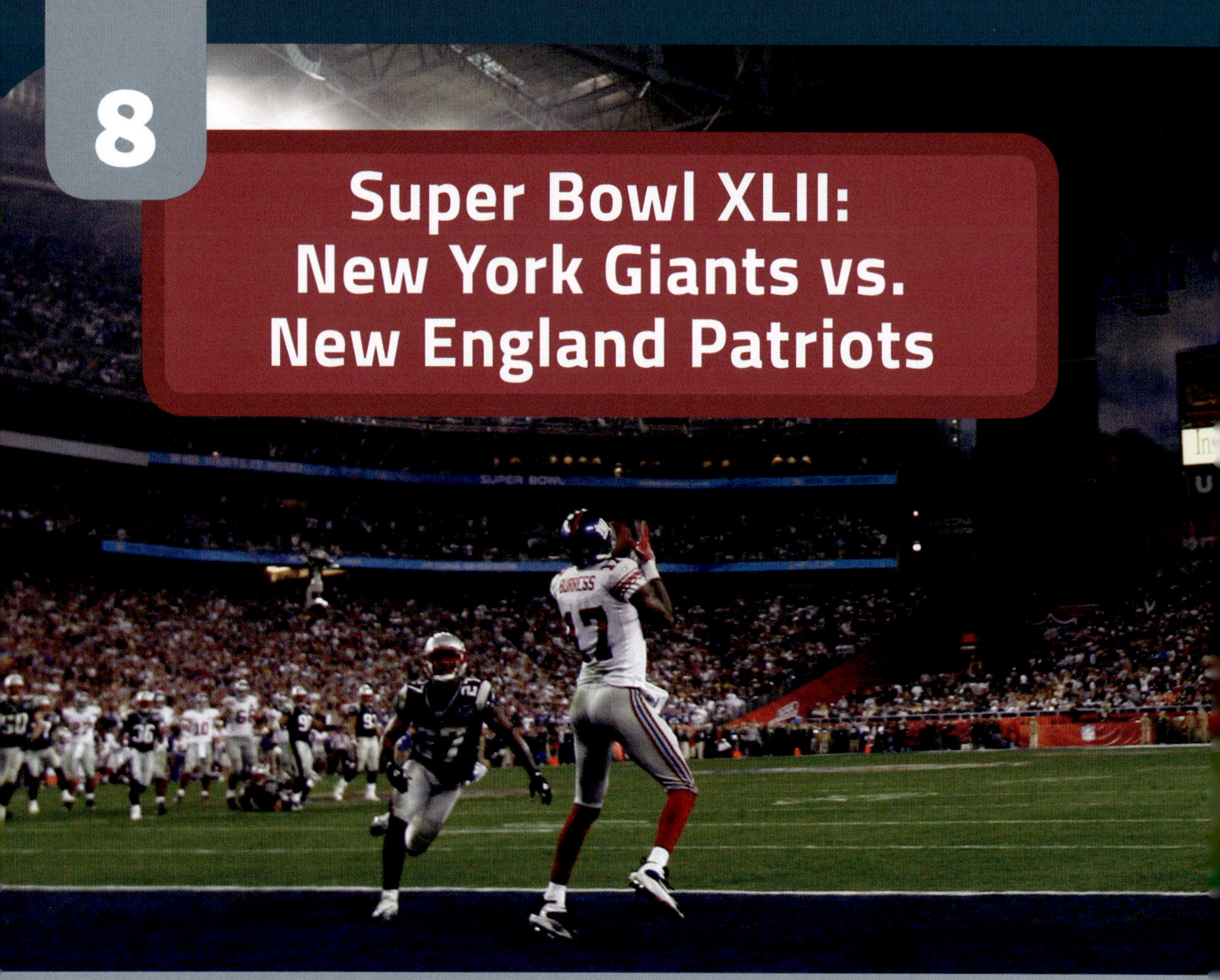


Maybe it was the helmet catch. Maybe it was the defense. Quarterback Eli Manning and the New York Giants pulled off a huge Super Bowl upset in 2008 at Super Bowl XLII. The New England Patriots were aiming for a perfect no-losses season. Only the Miami Dolphins had finished a Super Bowl season with an unbeaten record.

The Giants stole the Super Bowl show. Manning won it with a touchdown pass to Plaxico Burress. The play came with 35 seconds left. It is one of the most famous plays in Super Bowl history. It set up the winning touchdown. David Tyree caught a pass from Manning. He held the ball against his helmet as he fell to the ground. The play gave the Giants a first down at the Patriots 24-yard line. The Giants scored. And won 17 to 14. Manning was named Super Bowl MVP.

## 5

**Number of sacks by the Giants of Patriots quarterback Tom Brady.**

- The Giants pulled off one of the biggest upsets in Super Bowl history.
- The Patriots entered the game with an unbeaten 18-0 record.
- Plaxico Burress caught a touchdown pass from Giants quarterback Eli Manning with 35 seconds left.
- Manning passed for 255 yards and two touchdowns. He was named MVP.

### PERFECTION

The New England Patriots failed to complete a perfect season in Super Bowl XLII. They were trying to become the second team to do so. In 1972, the Miami Dolphins won all 17 games they played. The Dolphins completed their perfect season with a 14-7 victory over the Washington Redskins in Super Bowl VII.

9

# Super Bowl XLIV: New Orleans Saints vs. Indianapolis Colts

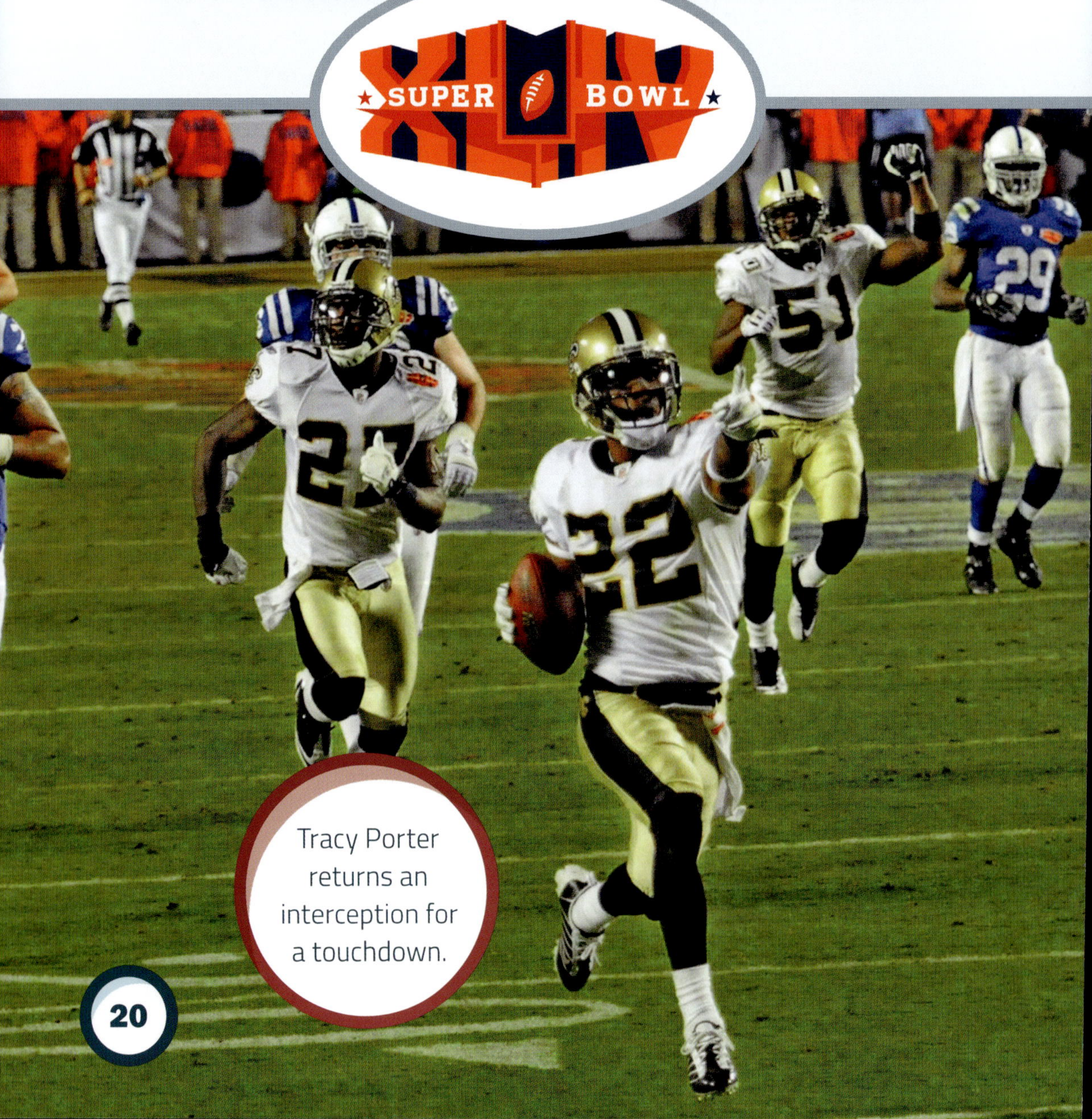


Tracy Porter returns an interception for a touchdown.

One glorious Super Bowl victory in 2010 punched life back into New Orleans. The city had suffered from a direct hit by Hurricane Katrina in 2005. The Saints had not had a winning season in years. That all changed in Super Bowl XLIV.

Saints quarterback Drew Brees passed for 288 yards and two touchdowns. The Saints scored 25 points in the second half. They knocked off the Indianapolis Colts, 31 to 17. It was the first Super Bowl game ever for the Saints.

The Saints began the second half with an onside kick attempt. They recovered the ball. The play set up a touchdown pass by Brees. The Saints scored the last 18 points of the game to pull away. Tracy Porter returned an interception 74 yards for a touchdown in the fourth quarter. The Colts were an NFL powerhouse in 2009 and heavily favored to win. They won their first 14 games behind quarterback Peyton Manning. Manning still was a big factor in the Super Bowl. He passed for 333 yards and one touchdown.

## THINK ABOUT IT

New Orleans had experienced tragedy with Hurricane Katrina. How do you think winning the Super Bowl helped the people of that city?

**32**

**Completions by Saints quarterback Drew Brees in Super Bowl XLIV.**

- Brees passed for 288 yards and two touchdowns. He was named Super Bowl MVP.
- The Saints scored 25 points in the second half to beat the Colts.
- Colts quarterback Peyton Manning passed for 333 yards.

10

# Super Bowl XLVII: Baltimore Ravens vs. San Francisco 49ers

Getting to the Super Bowl in 2013 was not easy for the Baltimore Ravens. The Ravens lost six games during the regular season. They had to win a wild card playoff game to move on. They won their last two playoff games on the road. And made it to the Super bowl. Then they had to wait out a power failure in the Super Bowl.

Ravens quarterback Jim Flacco celebrates the win.

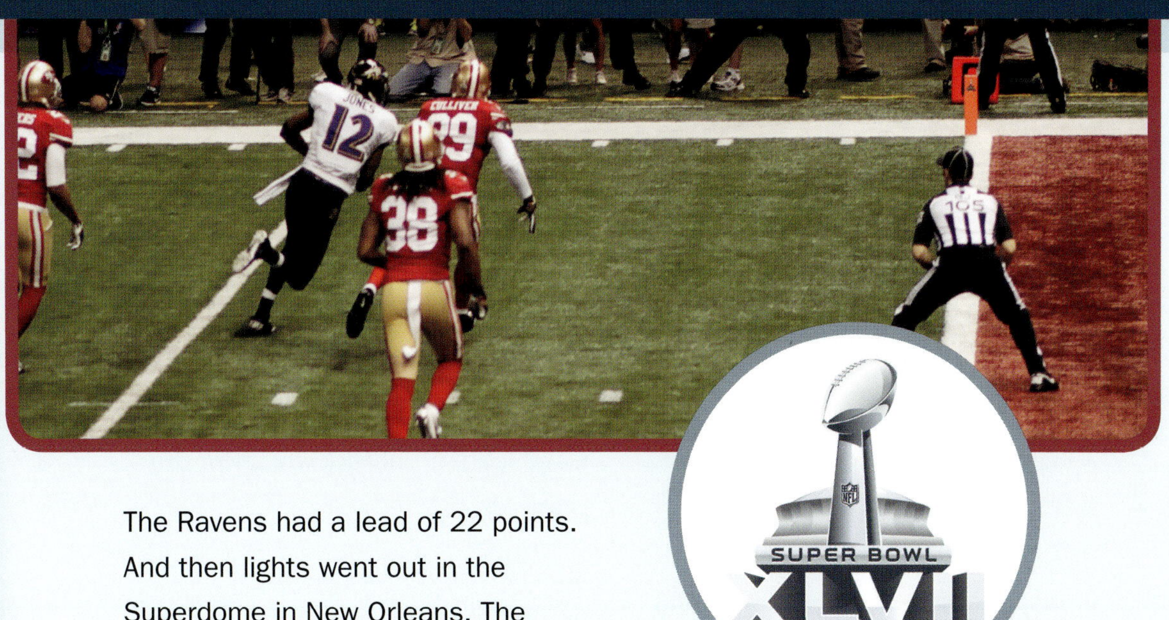


The Ravens had a lead of 22 points. And then lights went out in the Superdome in New Orleans. The power failure happened soon after Jacoby Jones of Baltimore returned the second half kickoff. It was a touchdown for 108 yards.

The Ravens defeated the 49ers. But the win still didn't come easy for the Ravens. The 49ers almost rallied from 22 points down. The Ravens did not score a touchdown after the kickoff return by Jones. The 49ers outscored the Ravens 25-6 in the second half of the game. But the Ravens held on and won 34-31.

Ravens quarterback Jim Flacco was making his Super Bowl debut. He passed for 287 yards and three touchdowns. He was named game MVP. Ravens coach Jim Harbaugh defeated his brother, John, who was coach of the 49ers.

# 164

**Combined yards in two touchdowns scored by Jacoby Jones of the Baltimore Ravens.**

- Ravens beat the 49ers by three points.
- Ravens quarterback Jim Flacco won the game MVP.
- Flacco passed for 287 yards and three touchdowns.
- The game was the first match up of brothers. Both head coaches of opposing teams.

# 11

# Super Bowl XLVIII: Seattle Seahawks vs. Denver Broncos

A nightmare began on the very first play for the Denver Broncos. It was 2014. The Broncos lined up on offense to begin the game following the kickoff. Broncos center Manny Ramirez snapped the ball back to quarterback Peyton Manning. He wasn't ready. The ball sailed over his head and into the end zone for a safety. The Seattle Seahawks took a 2-0 lead. It only got worse for the Broncos.

Malcolm Smith was a linebacker for the Seattle Seahawks. He intercepted a Manning pass in the second quarter. And returned it 69 yards for a touchdown. That play made it 22 to 0. Seahawks Percy Harvey returned the second half

**4**

**Number of turnovers by the Denver Broncos in Super Bowl XLVIII.**

- The Seattle Seahawks scored a safety on the first play of the game.
- Malcolm Smith returned an interception 69 yards for a touchdown. He was named MVP.
- Percy Harvey returned a kickoff for an 87-yard touchdown.
- Broncos quarterback Peyton Manning was intercepted twice and sacked once.

kickoff 87 yards for a touchdown. The Seahawks wound up winning by a score of 43 to 8. It was the most lopsided Super Bowl in more than 20 years.

Both teams entered Super Bowl XLVIII with 15-3 records. But Denver was an offensive powerhouse. The Broncos broke the NFL record for points scored in the regular season. Denver scored 606 points. Manning passed for 5,477 yards. He passed for 55 touchdowns. Both were the highest of his career.

The final score was shocking. Manning passed for 280 yards and one touchdown. But he was intercepted twice. Smith had one interception. He recovered a fumble. He became one of the few defensive players to win Super Bowl MVP.

12

# Super Bowl 50: Denver Broncos vs. Carolina Panthers

The Carolina Panthers had lost just one game all season. Panthers quarterback Cam Newton passed for 35 touchdowns during the regular season. He passed for 3,837 yards. He was named NFL MVP of the NFL season.

The Denver Broncos ruined the Super Bowl party for Newton in 2016. The Denver defense dominated the Panthers. They sacked Newton six times in a 24-10 victory. The only Panthers touchdown came on a 1-yard run by Jonathan Stewart.

Von Miller retrieves the ball from Cam Newton for a touchdown.

Newton was intercepted once. The Panthers lost three fumbles. Newton completed 18 of 41 passes for 265 yards.

It was the last game for Broncos quarterback Peyton Manning. And his second Super Bowl win. The biggest star was Broncos linebacker Von Miller. He had two and a half sacks. He forced two fumbles. Miller was named Super Bowl MVP.

## 4

**Number of turnovers by the Carolina Panthers.**

- The Broncos handed the Carolina Panthers their second loss of the season.
- The Broncos had a dominating defensive performance.
- Von Miller of the Broncos was named MVP.
- Broncos quarterback Peyton Manning won his second Super Bowl championship. It was his final game.

## THINK ABOUT IT

Peyton Manning was almost 40 years old when he played in Super Bowl 50. He retired shortly after. Do you think that he chose the right time to retire? Why or why not?

# Fun Facts and Stories

## Hometown Title

Jerome Bettis returned to his hometown of Detroit to win his only Super Bowl. It was the final game of his NFL career. Bettis was born in Detroit on February 16, 1972. He was a running back for the Pittsburgh Steelers. Bettis rushed for 43 yards in Super Bowl XL. The Steelers won the game played at Ford Field in Detroit, 21-10. There were tears on the Steelers sideline. They knew it was Bettis' last game. Bettis called himself the luckiest football player ever.

## Remember Me?

Jon Gruden accomplished a first in Super Bowl XXXVII. And then some. He became the first coach to leave a team and coach against it the following year. He had been coach of the Oakland Raiders. In 2003, he led the Tampa Bay Bucs to a Super Bowl win against the Raiders. It was the first Super Bowl win in Tampa Bay history. He started as an assistant coach at age 27. He did not have furniture in his apartment. He slept in the San Francisco 49ers coaching office.

## Brother, Brother

The Baltimore Ravens and San Francisco 49ers produced a unique brotherly conflict in Super Bowl XLVII. The game marked the first time that two brothers were the opposing head coaches. Jim Harbaugh led his Ravens to a 34-31 win over John Harbaugh and the 49ers. They met on the field after the game. Jim patted his brother on the cheek. John told Jim he loved him.

## The Big Game

Bill Belichick has played a part in Super Bowl history on both sides of the field. He was the defensive coordinator for the New York Giants. They defeated the Buffalo Bills in Super Bowl XXV in 1991. He was the New England Patriots head coach 17 years later. The Giants knocked off his unbeaten Patriots in Super Bowl XLII. It was the first time he lost a Super Bowl game.

## Retirement Talk

Star quarterback Peyton Manning wasn't sure if he would retire after Super Bowl 50. Tony Dungy was his former coach with the Indianapolis Colts. He talked to Dungy about retiring. Dungy advised Manning not to make an emotional decision. The Broncos won Super Bowl 50. It wasn't until a month later that Manning announced it was his last game. He retired a Super Bowl champ.

## Number One and Two

Super Bowl 50 featured a matchup between the top two picks in the 2011 NFL Draft. Carolina Panthers quarterback Cam Newton was the number one pick in the draft. Denver Broncos Linebacker Von Miller was the second player chosen. Miller played four years at Texas A&M. Newton played two seasons at Florida and then one year at Auburn.

# Glossary

**debut**
The first time a player performs in a game or a team plays in a Super Bowl.

**field goal**
When a player kicks the ball between the two uprights in the goal post. A field goal scores three points.

**Hall of Fame**
An organization that recognizes outstanding players. Players are eligible to be voted into the Hall of Fame after retirement.

**interception**
When a pass is caught by a player from the opposing team.

**kickoff**
The ball is placed in a kicking tee and kicked downfield to the other team. It is kicked at the start of the game and the second half. Kickoffs also happen after a touchdown or field goal.

**MVP**
Abbreviation for most valuable player.

**onside kick**
When the ball is kicked a short distance in an attempt to recover the ball. The ball must be kicked at least 10 yards in order for the play to count.

**quarterback**
A player who runs the offense. They take the ball on a snap from the center. The quarterback usually passes the ball or hands it off to a running back.

**sack**
When a defensive player tackles a quarterback in the backfield.

**safety**
When a player with the ball is tackled in their own end zone. Or a punt is blocked and goes out of their end zone. It's worth two points for the opposing team.

**upset**
When a team not expected to win actually does so.

**wild-card playoff**
When a team makes the playoffs because of their good win-loss record.

# For More Information

## Books

Howell, Brian, *12 Reasons to Love Football*, Mankato, MN: 12-Story Library, 2018.

Nichols, John, *NFL Today: The Story of the Pittsburgh Steelers*, NFL Today, Creative Company, 2011.

Wilner, Barry, The Super Bowl, SportsZone, Minneapolis, MN: Abdo Publishing, 2013.

# Index



## About the Author

Paul Bowker is an editor and author who lives on Cape Cod in South Yarmouth, Massachusetts. His 35-year newspaper career has included hundreds of NFL games. He is a national past president of Associated Press Sports Editors and has won multiple national writing awards.